Santa's Runaway Elf

by Jean Lewis
Illustrated by Marjorie Cooper

Brown Watson
ENGLAND

TINY Elf longed for the day he'd be big enough to go to the North Pole to be one of Santa's helpers.

"It's the most fun ever!" the bigger elves told him. "Wait and see!"

But Tiny couldn't wait another minute, so he hitched a ride on a shooting star and made a soft landing in a snowbank.

He looked around. Was this the North Pole, or was he lost?

Then he heard a deep kindly voice ask, "Are you lost, little fella?"

It was Santa!

Tiny took a deep breath. "I want to be one
of your helpers, Santa. I know I'm small, but
I promise I'll work hard and grow fast!"

The old man chuckled. "First, meet two

members of my team."

"Dancer and Prancer!" gasped Tiny.

"Right!" laughed Santa as the reindeer
pranced and danced for Tiny.

Santa gave each one a sugar lump. The reindeer shook their antlers in delight as they pranced off.

Then Santa sat down on a log and took
Tiny on his knee.

"Suppose you visit all my workshops," said
Santa. "Then pick out the job you think you
can do best."

Tiny's first stop was the Carpentry Shop.
He climbed on a bench to see.

Everywhere grown-up elves were busy sawing
and hammering, making all kinds of wonderful
toys for Christmas.

"Don't step on those nails, boy," said an elf. "I've got thirty more ladders to finish by midnight!"

Tiny saw the elves' tools were much too big. This wasn't the job for him.

In the Paint Shop Tiny watched elves carefully painting blue eyes and grey spots on a white rocking horse.

Tiny knew if that horse didn't look just right, some youngster was going to be very disappointed. He left.

Tiny didn't stay long at the Doll Dressmaking Shop either.

"You're a perfect size one!" cried one of the ladies.

But Tiny hadn't come to the North Pole to be a doll dressmaker's dummy!

The little elf was feeling pretty discouraged. Would he ever find the job he could do best?

Suddenly, he smelled something—something delicious!

"Come in!" called Mrs. Santa. "Taste my

new candy canes!"

"*Yum-mee!*" exclaimed Tiny.

He longed to stay and taste all the Christmas
treats in Mrs. Santa's kitchen. But he must
keep on job hunting.

Then Tiny had an idea. "I'll make a job for myself. I'll make Christmas cards!"

At the North Pole Library he looked through books of poems and pictures.

Finally, Tiny made up a Christmas card of his own.

"Wait till Santa sees this!" he said.

But when he showed Santa his card, the
old man shook his head.

"Tiny, I'm afraid you haven't learned to
spell or draw well enough yet to make
Christmas cards."

And the wise old man told Tiny to stop and take a "snow break."

So Tiny ran outside and built the biggest, jolliest snowman ever.

"Now for the last workshop," said Tiny. "I know I'll find a job there!"

The last workshop was full of trucks,
planes and trains.

Professor Willy Elf launched a toy spaceship
just for Tiny.

"Please, may I work here?" asked Tiny.

"Do you have a diploma from Engineering
School?" asked the Professor.

Tiny didn't even have a Nursery School
diploma. Outside he met some elves hauling a
sledge full of panda bears.

"Can I help?" he asked.

"Sure," they said. "Hang onto this rope
while we clear a path."

But the sledge was too heavy for Tiny. It skidded downhill, dumping all the toy pandas in the snow.

The elves were very cross. "Go away!" they told Tiny. "You're no help!"

Blinded by tears, Tiny ran right into Santa.
"I'm no good for any job here!" sobbed the
little elf.

"There's nothing wrong with you that won't
be right in a year," said Santa. "Then you'll
be big enough and smart enough to be one of my
best helpers."

"Honest?" said Tiny, drying his eyes.

"Right now there's a job that just fits you. Come on!" said Santa. "It's almost time for take-off!"

On their way to the reindeer stables, Santa told Tiny how he longed for company on his Christmas Eve rides.

MERRIE

CHRISTMAS

"Every inch on my sleigh is needed for toys,"
said Santa. "But you're small enough to perch
on my shoulder!"

Mrs. Santa and all the helpers came to
give Tiny and Santa a big send-off.

And that's how Santa's Runaway Elf came home on Christmas Eve.

"See you next year!" called Santa.

Tiny waved. "A year isn't so long—if you spend it growing!" said Tiny.

"Merry Christmas!"